To Crow Or Not To Crow?

Written and Illustrated by Carolee Carrara

"To Crow Or Not To Crow" is dedicated to my dear children, grandchildren and great grandchildren ... my gifts from God.

I am eternally grateful for divine inspiration from my Lord and Saviour, Jesus Christ.

My heartfelt thanks to my dear husband Romeo for his neverending support and encouragement in the creation of this book.

With the rising of the sun a new day had begun,
A gift from God to you and me - to everyone.
Roostie the Rooster threw his head back and stood up tall,
Crowing "Cock-a-doodle-doo and a good day to all!"

Farmer Jim fired up the tractor and headed for the fields.

It was another hard working day with lots of land to till.

The hens clucked and layed eggs in their nests.

The cows gave lots of milk and then took a nice rest.

Today a school bus is bringing the children to see
How important the farm is to our community.
They'll see the growing corn, apples, peas and more.
They'll get to see where food lives, before it goes to the store.

"Here they come!" says Farmer Jim, as the bus pulls in.
The children came running followed by Roostie and his friends.
With smiles on their faces, looking happy as can be,
The children love the farm! There's so much to see.

Farmer Jim took everyone to see the happy cows,
And little cups of fresh milk were passed around.
Jim said, "The cows are very important to you and me.
Without a glass of milk - how good would a cookie be?"

The children all received a cookie fresh from the kitchen,
And walked on to see the cute little chickens.
Farmer Jim praised the hens. There were eggs in every nest.
"You all deserve Blue Ribbons!" he said. "You are the best!"

Roostie listened closely and followed Farmer Jim,
Who kept praising the sheep, the goats and the hens.
He praised the ducks, the horses, the llamas and even the hogs.
Roostie hoped to hear praise for himself - but he did not.

When the tour was over, everyone ran to the bus.
The children were happy they had learned so much.
They hollered "Goodbye," and "Thank you, Farmer Jim!"
Roostie lifted his wing to wave, but no one noticed him.

He felt very sad - and kind of mad too.

He thought, "All I can do is crow - one silly, simple tune."

"Cock-a-doodle-doo," he mumbled as he walked away.

"I'm worthless! Useless! I can't even lay an egg!"

The next morning Roostie ignored the rising sun.
Everyone slept in. No work was getting done.
The farm was quiet. No mooing cows - no clucking hens.
There was no one awake in Roostie's pen.

"Wakeup!" Farmer Jim pounded on Roostie's door.

"What's going on? Why aren't you crowing anymore?"

But there was no answer coming from the coop.

"The farm's not right without Roostie. What am I gonna do?"

The next morning Roostie didn't crow AGAIN!
The alarm clock woke Farmer Jim, but everyone else slept in.
It was hard waking them up - but by the end of the day,
The cows gave a little milk, and the hens layed a few eggs.

Ruby the Hen went to see Roostie - to find out why he didn't crow.

"What made you stop?" she asked. "Everyone wants to know."

Roostie sighed, "Farmer Jim praised everyone but me.

To be honest, Ruby, I feel just as worthless as can be."

"Oh no," said Ruby. And she spoke from her heart.
"Without your cock-a-doodle-doo our farm is falling apart.
God gave all of us gifts - that are important to share.
Your crowing is special. We really need you here."

Roostie went to his bed later that night,
Thinking "To crow or not to crow? What would be right?
Ruby says I have a special gift - that I should crow ...
I think I'll sleep on it ... (big yawn) - I just don't know."

He fell asleep. Then suddenly was awakened by loud, clucking sounds.
He looked outside his coop and saw a fox sniffing around!
The fox was wily and cunning and up to no good.
Roostie knew he had to protect the hens. He had to do what he could!

He gave a fierce rooster growl and loudly proclaimed,
"Cock-A-Doodle-Doo!" and the fox ran away.
Farmer Jim came running and saw the fox jump the fence.
"Roostie you're a hero!" he said. "You saved all the hens!"

The hens gathered around Roostie and gave lots of hugs.
Roostie had never felt so important - and so loved.
They celebrated joyfully - one and all.
Roostie just beamed and stood up real tall.

He woke up the next morning with the rising of the sun.

Knowing he had a gift to share - with everyone.

He said to himself, "Roostie, do what you were born to do!"

Then gave out his loudest and best ever, "Cock-A-Doodle-Doo!"

"Each of us should use whatever gift we have received to serve others."

1 Peter 4:10

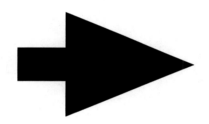

Coloring Page

Made in the USA
Middletown, DE
19 October 2022